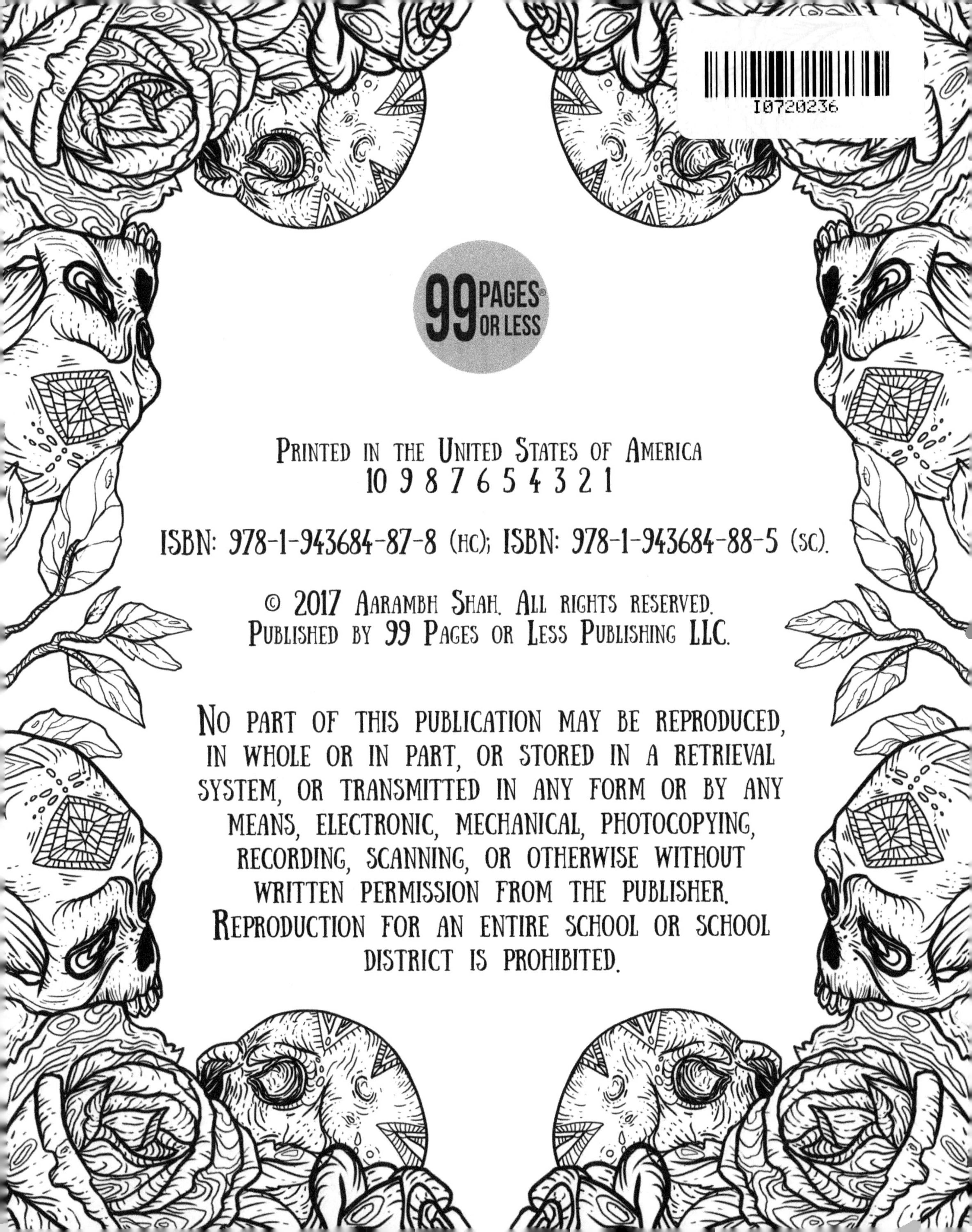

99 **PAGES** OR LESS

PRINTED IN THE UNITED STATES OF AMERICA
10 9 8 7 6 5 4 3 2 1

ISBN: 978-1-943684-87-8 (HC); ISBN: 978-1-943684-88-5 (SC).

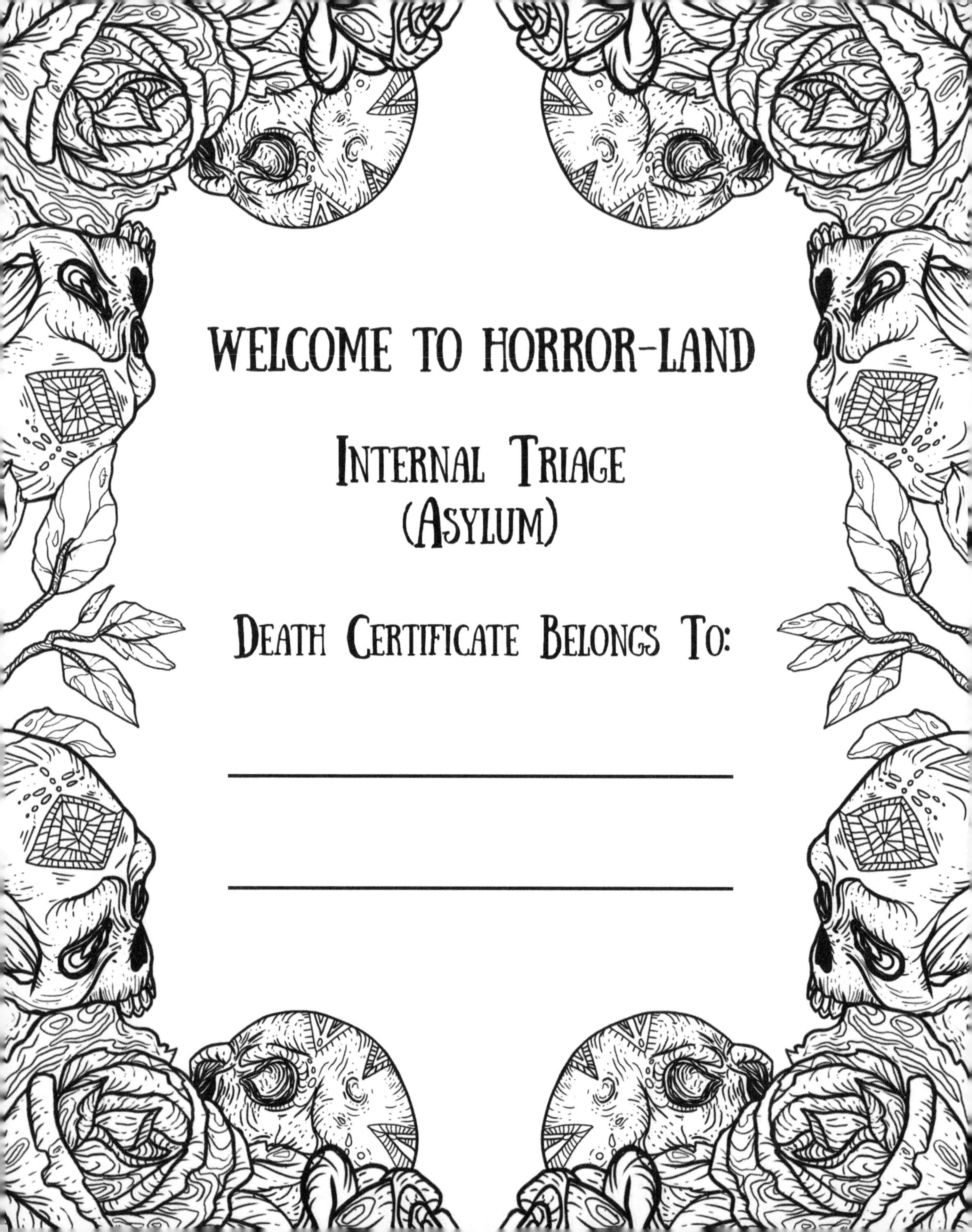

WELCOME TO HORROR-LAND

INTERNAL TRIAGE
(ASYLUM)

DEATH CERTIFICATE BELONGS TO:

____

____

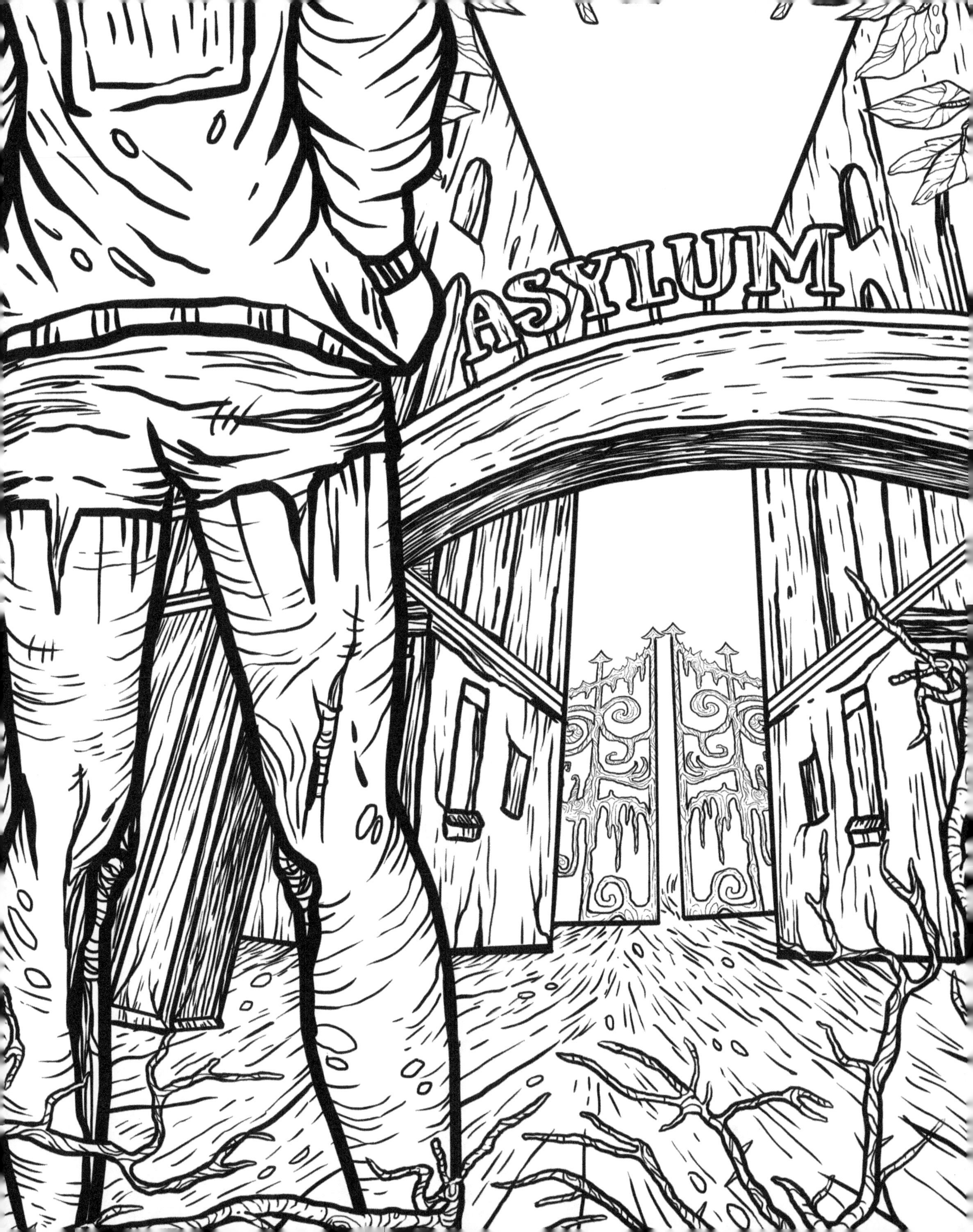

ASYLUM

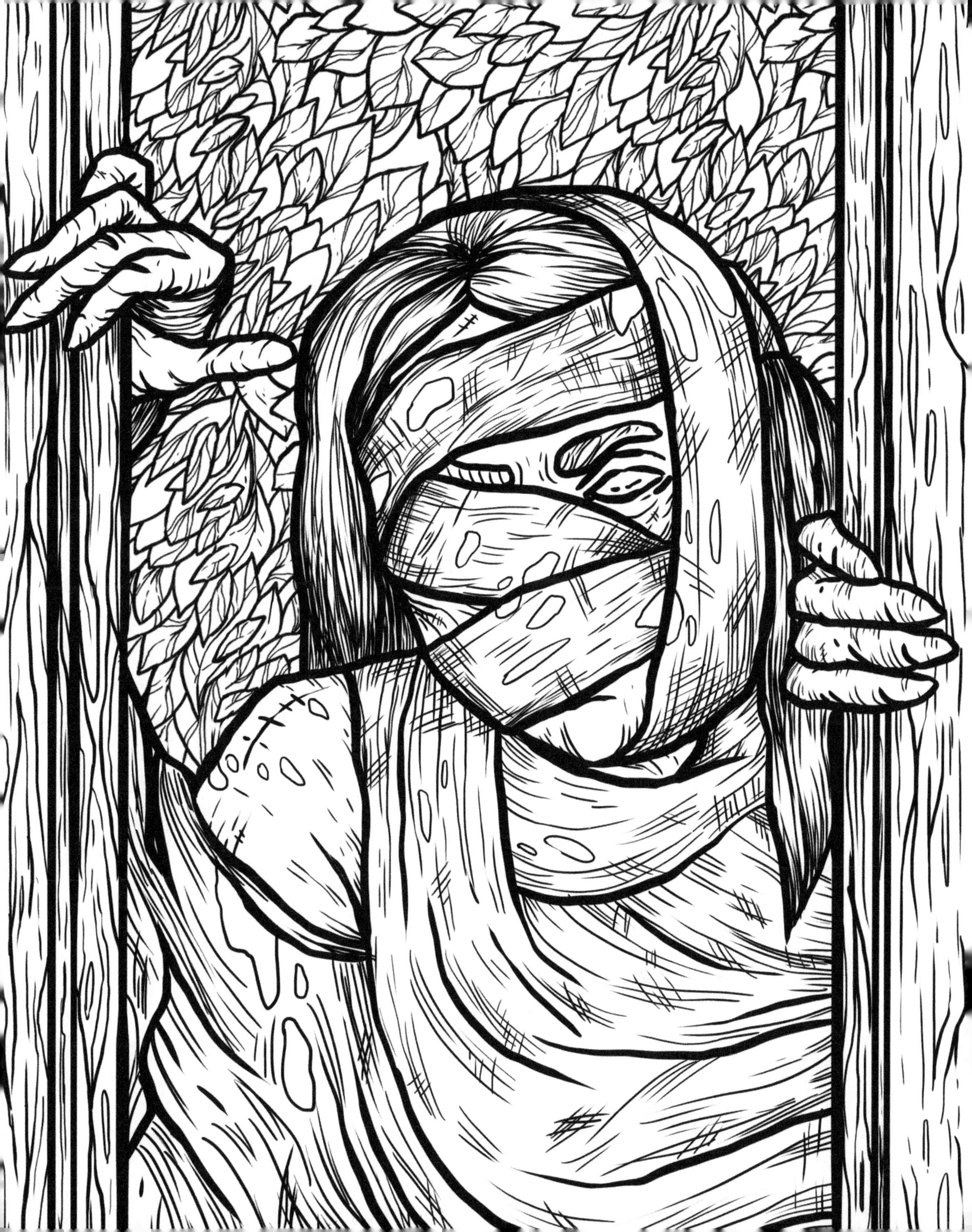

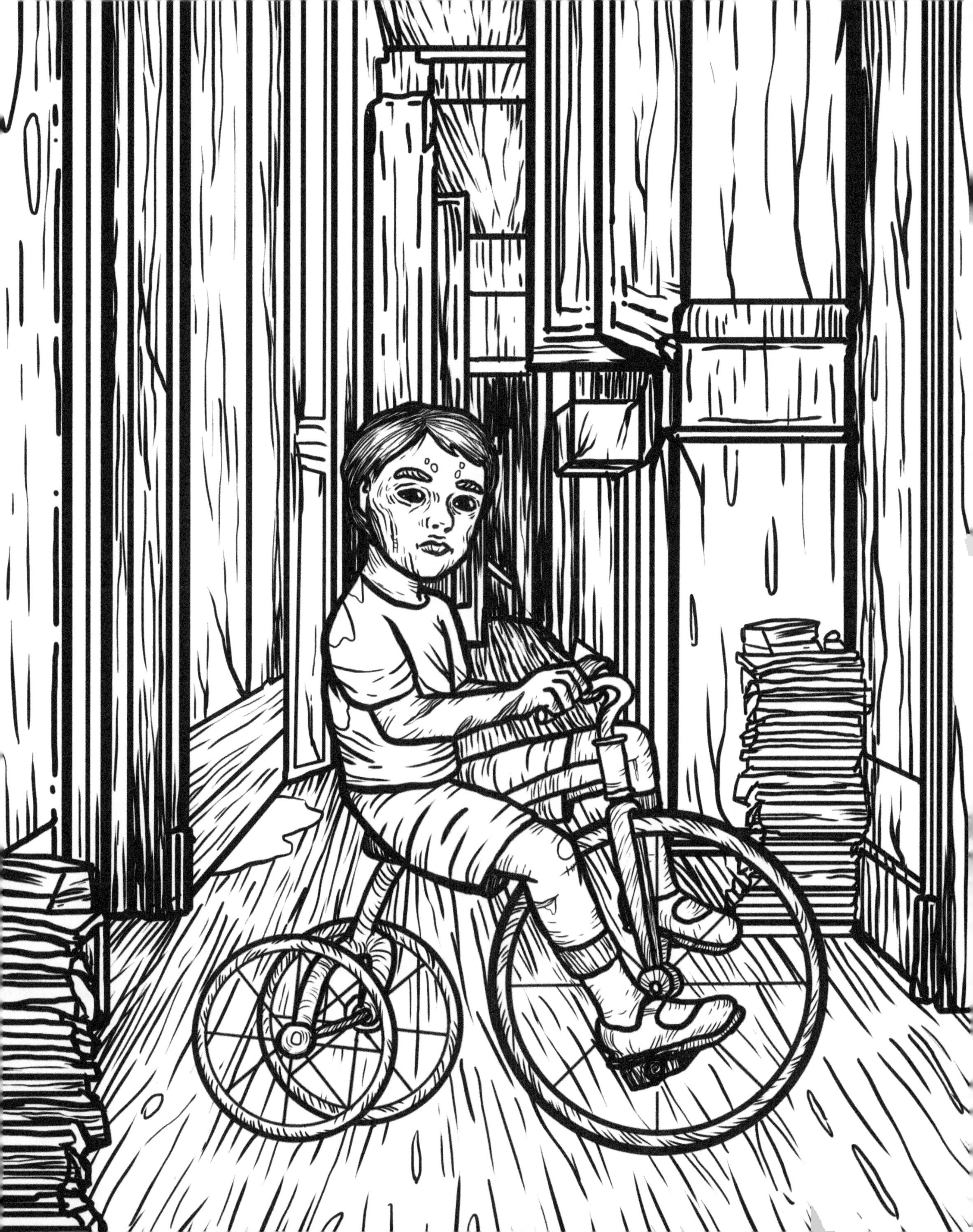

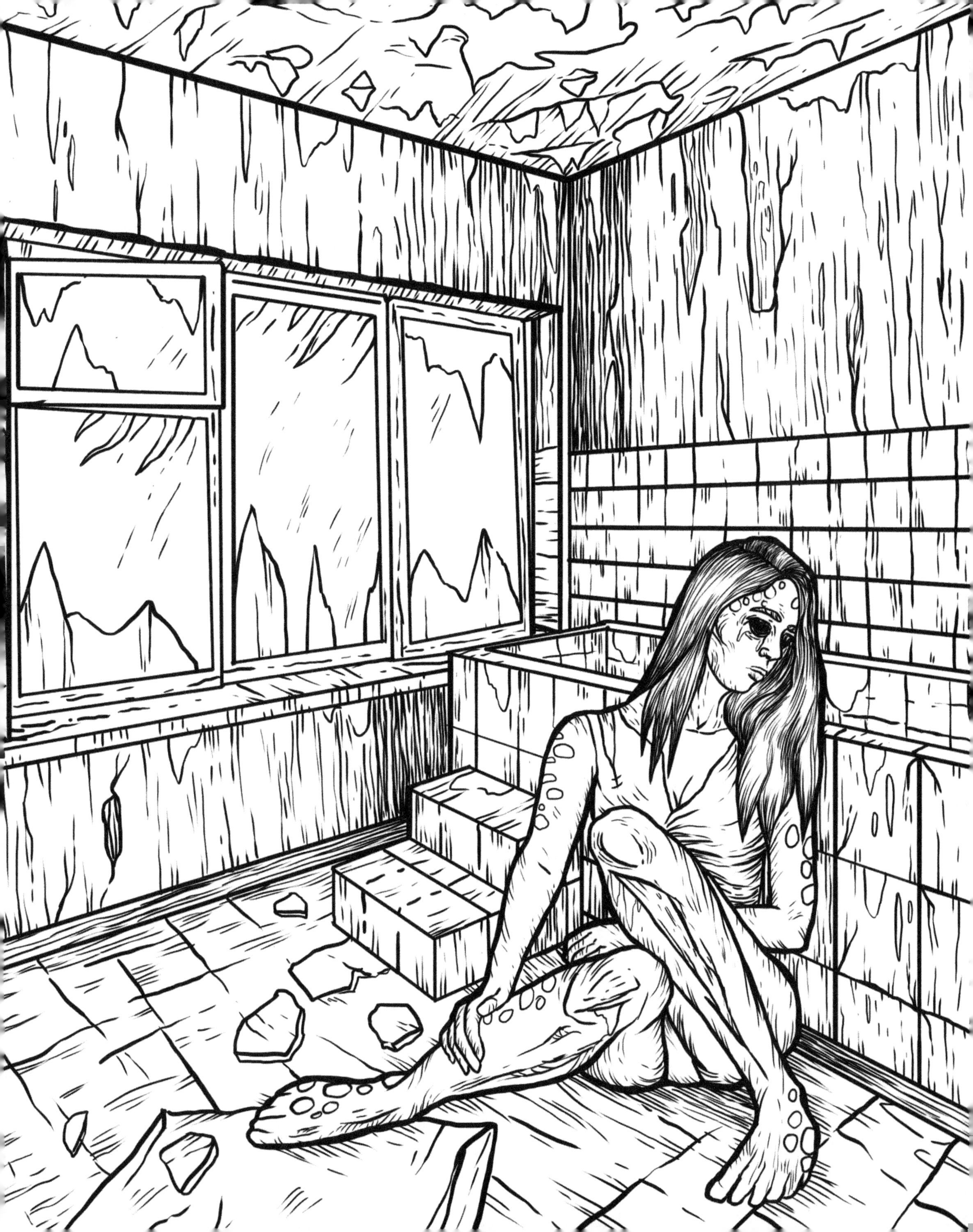

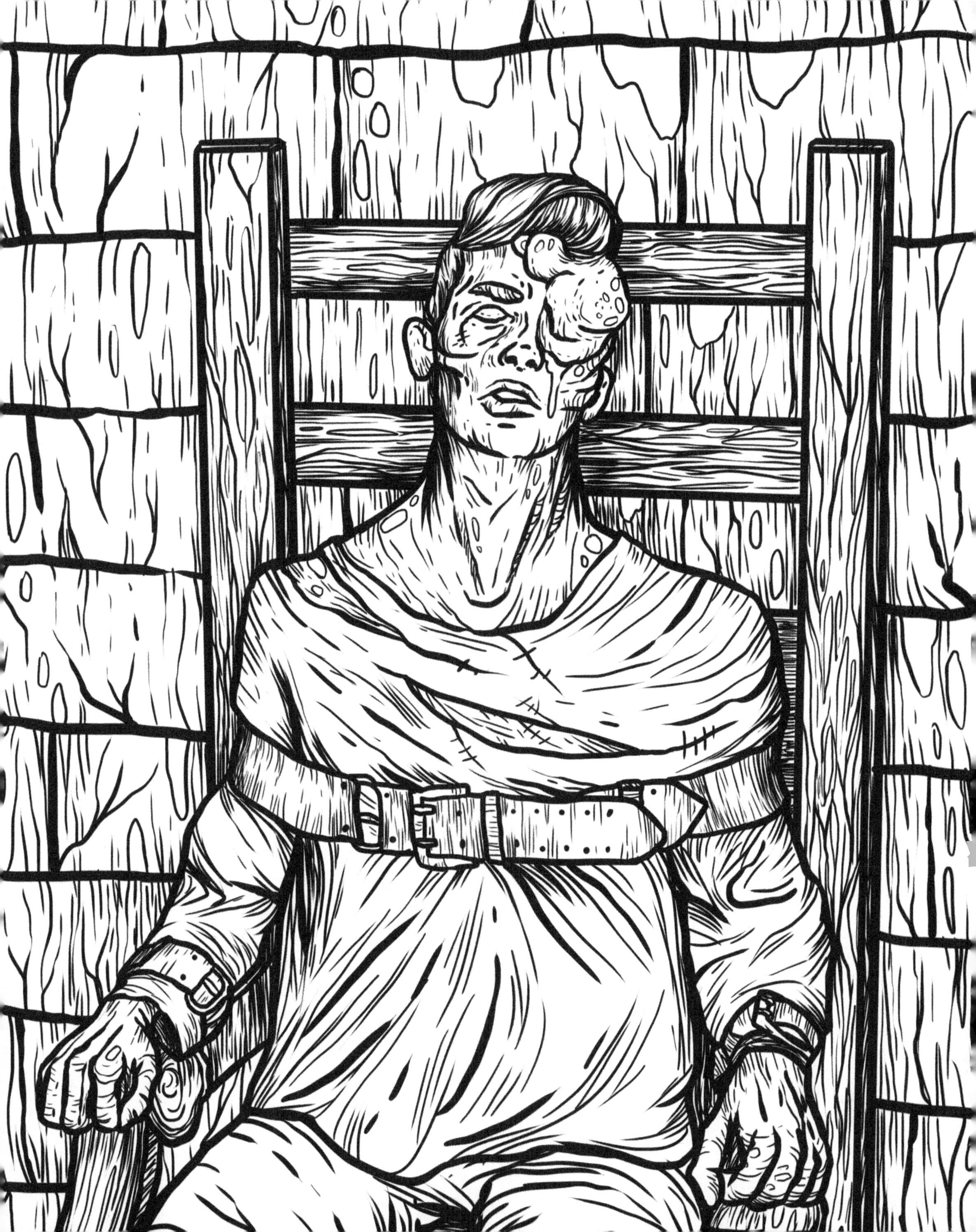

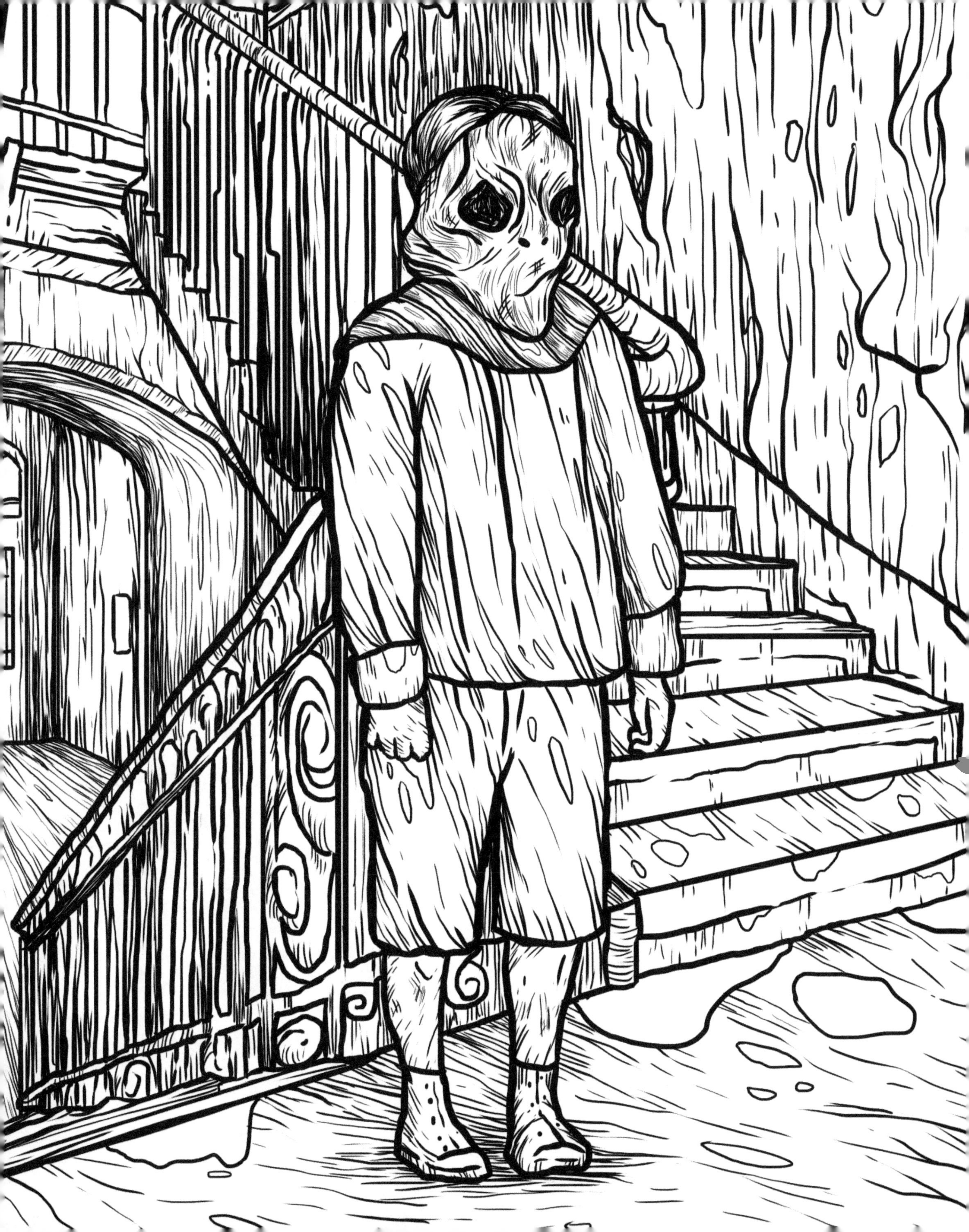

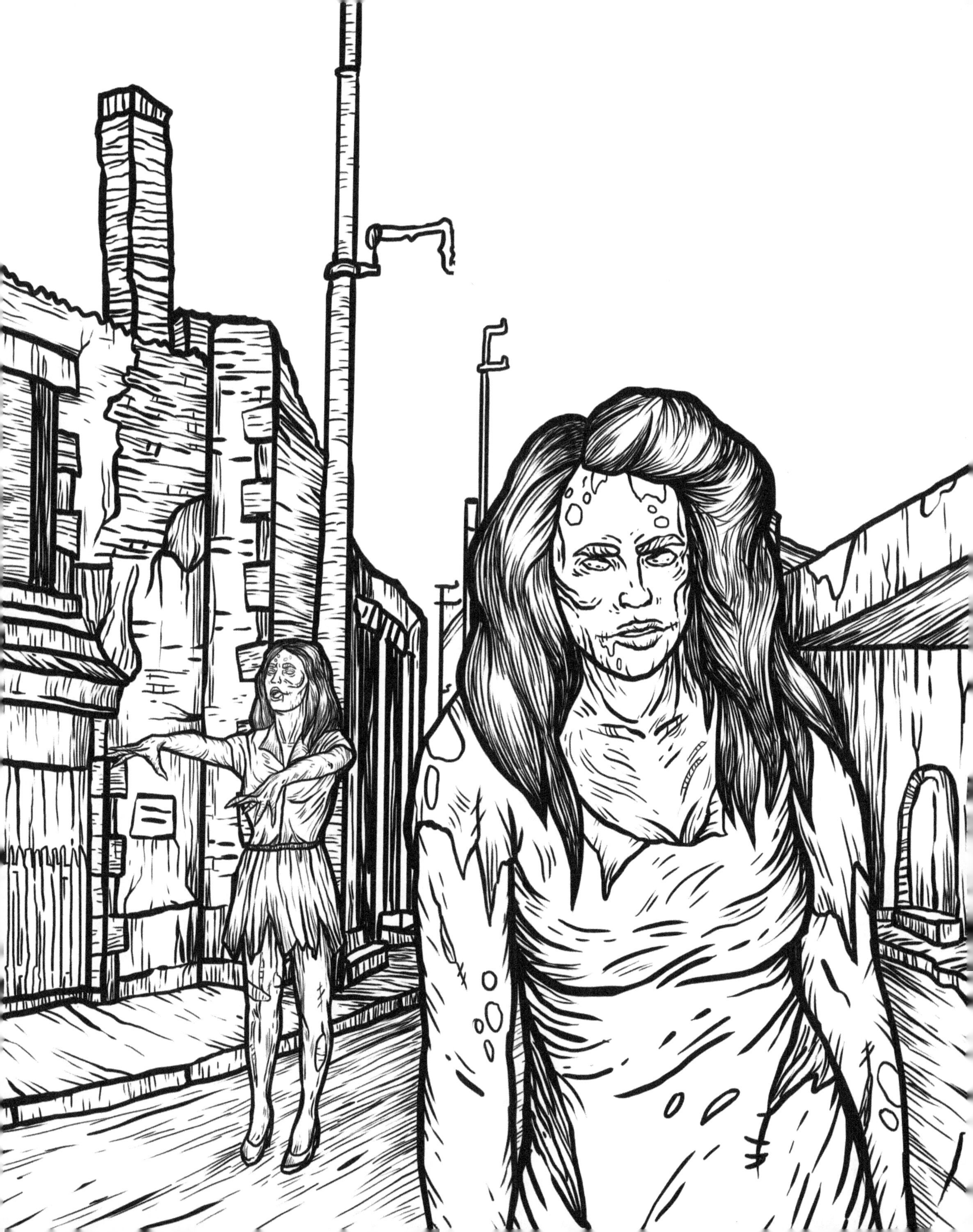

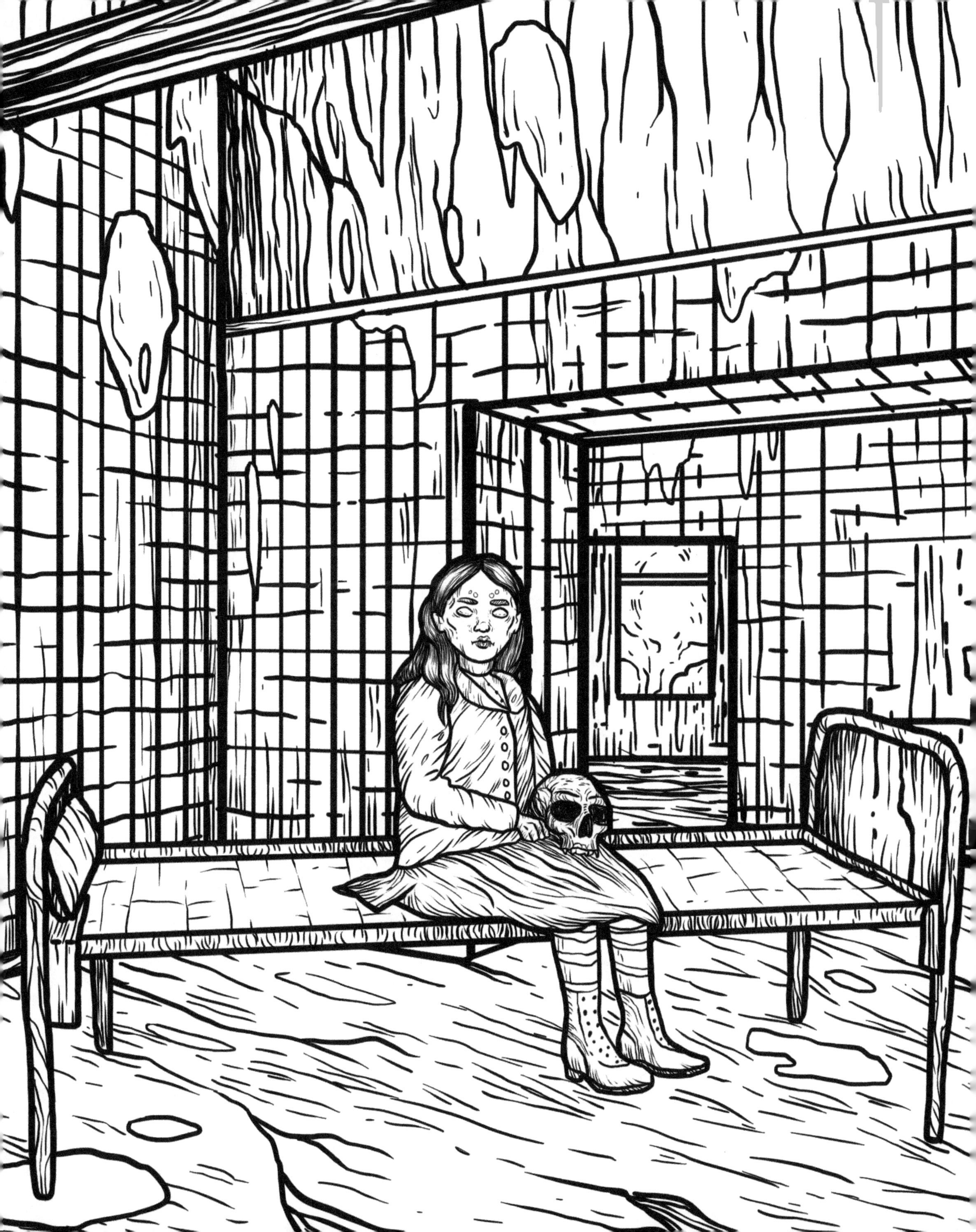

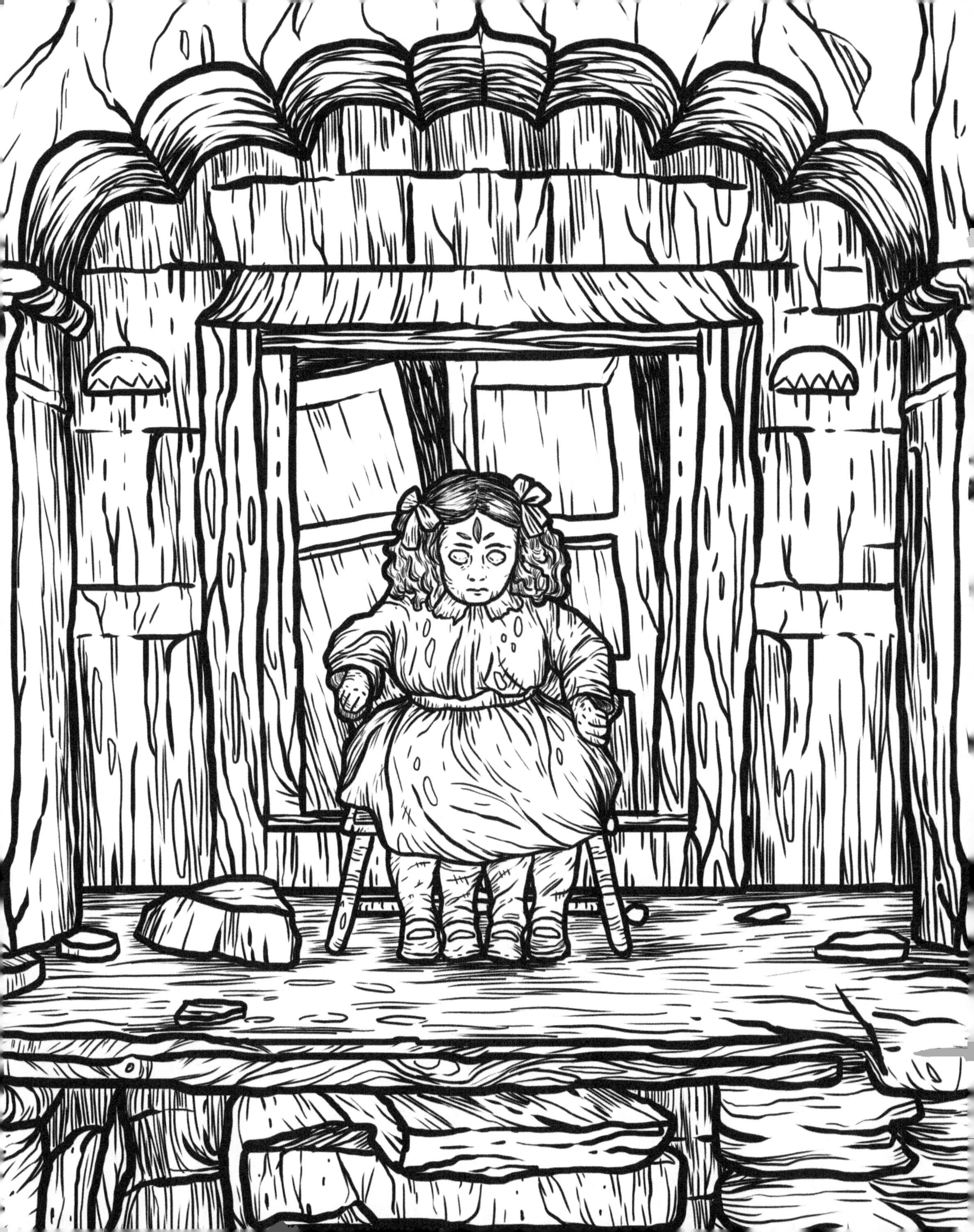

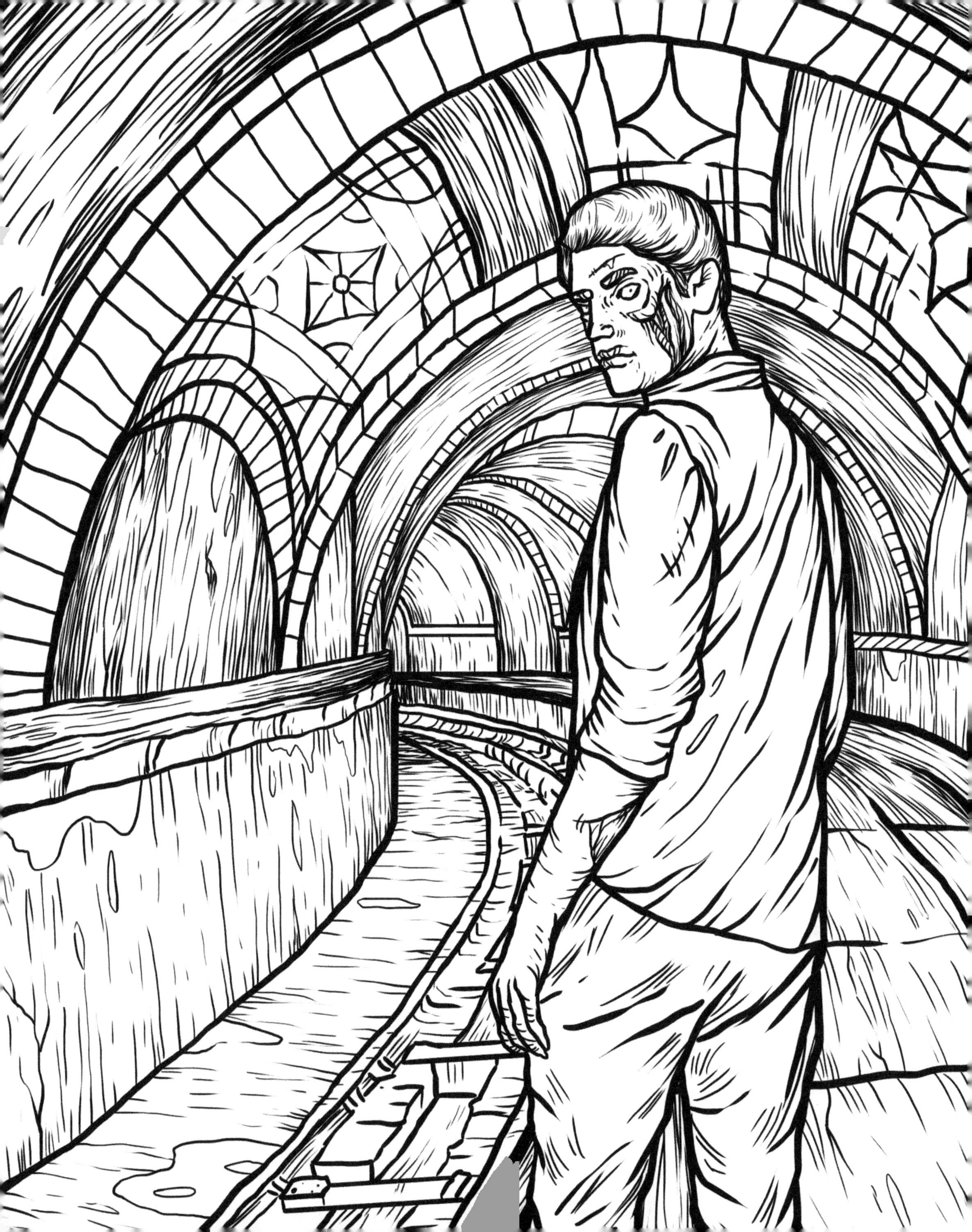

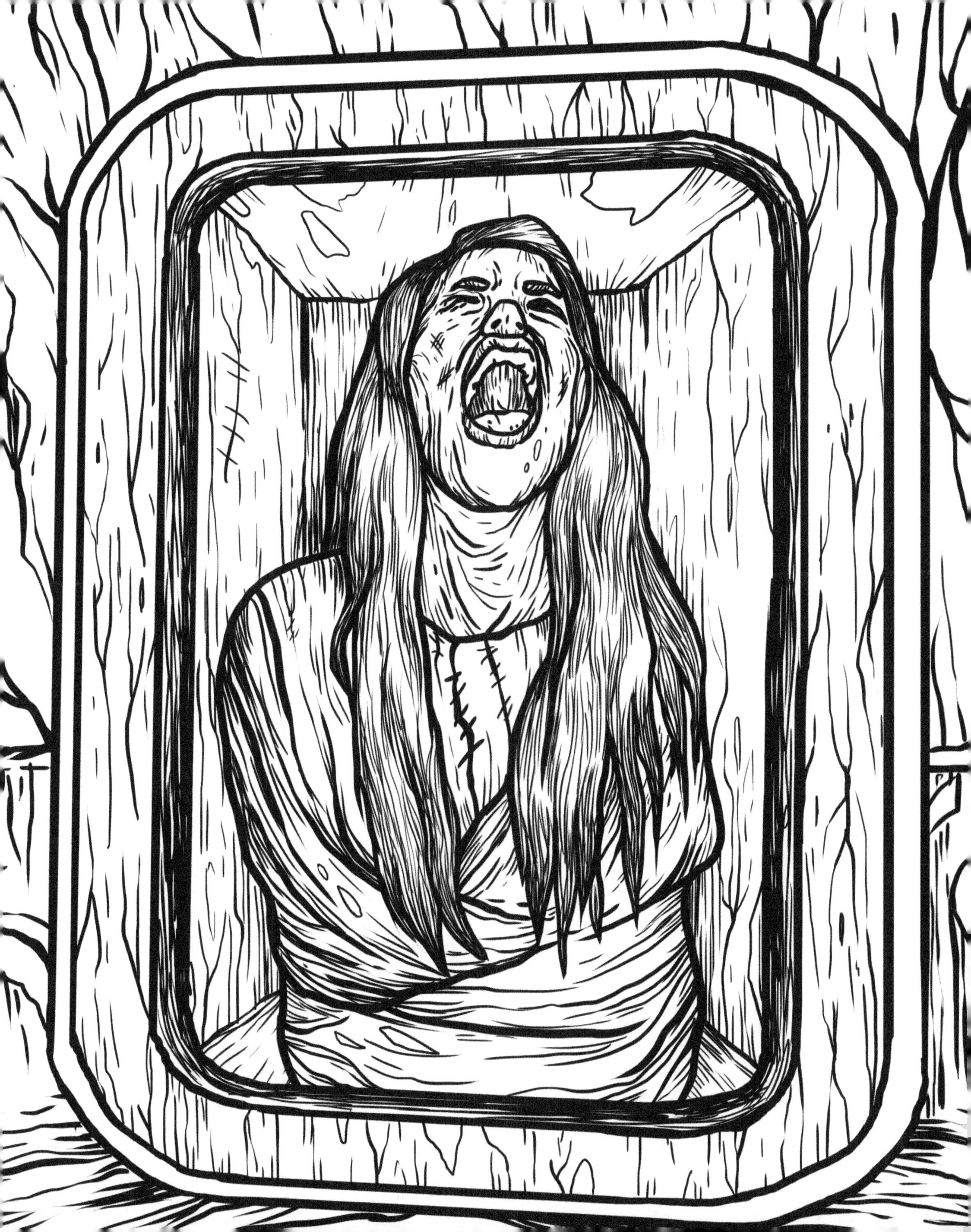

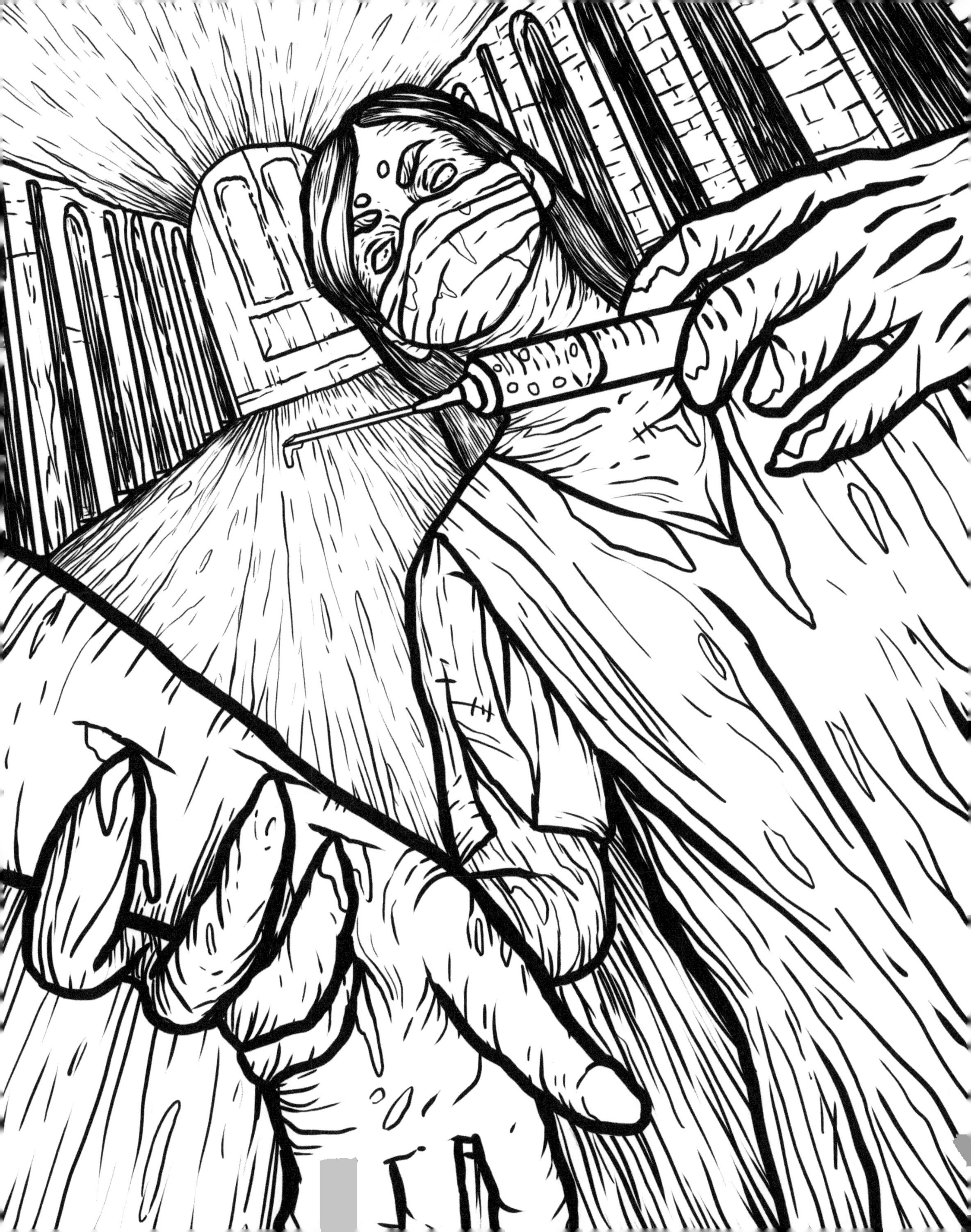

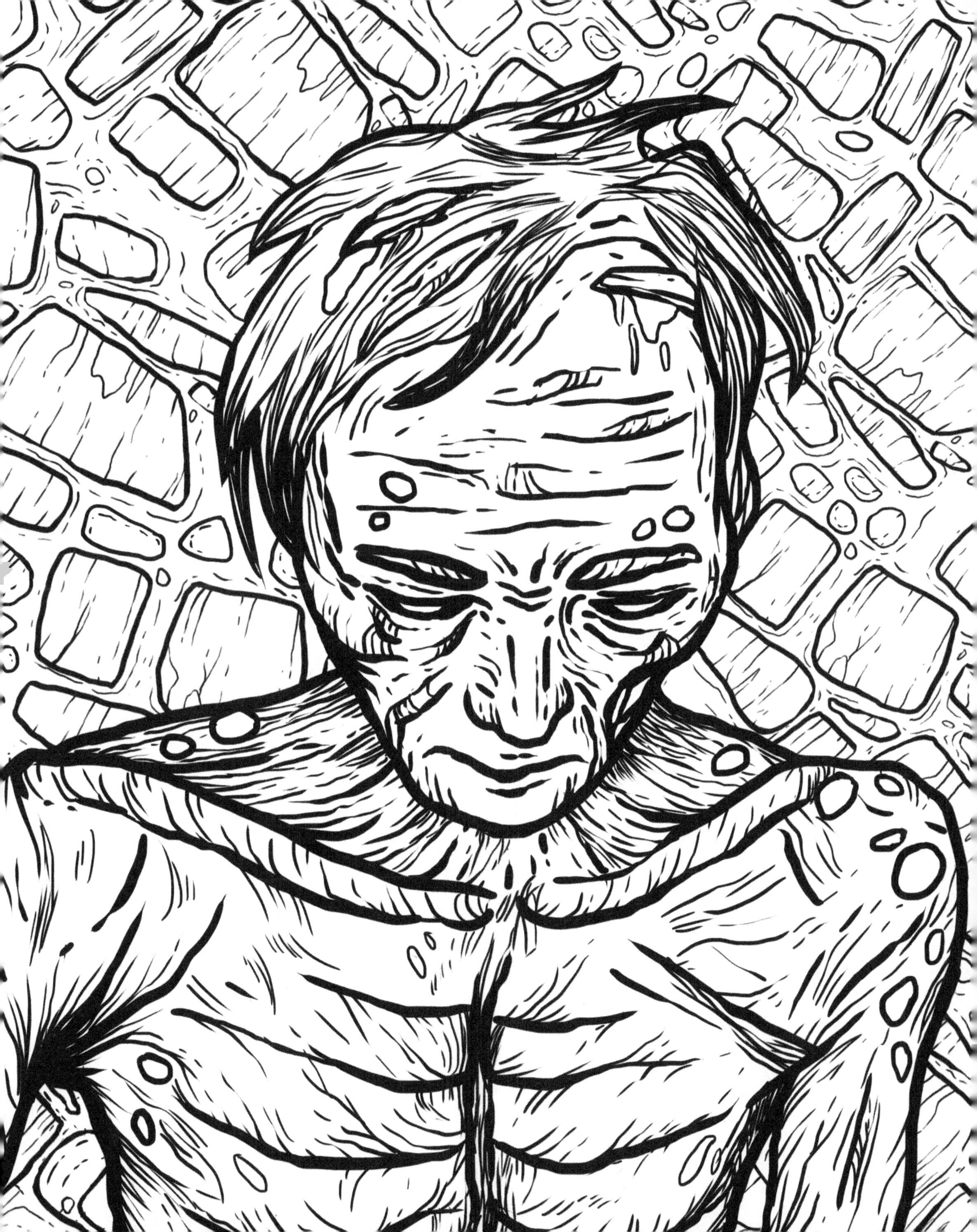

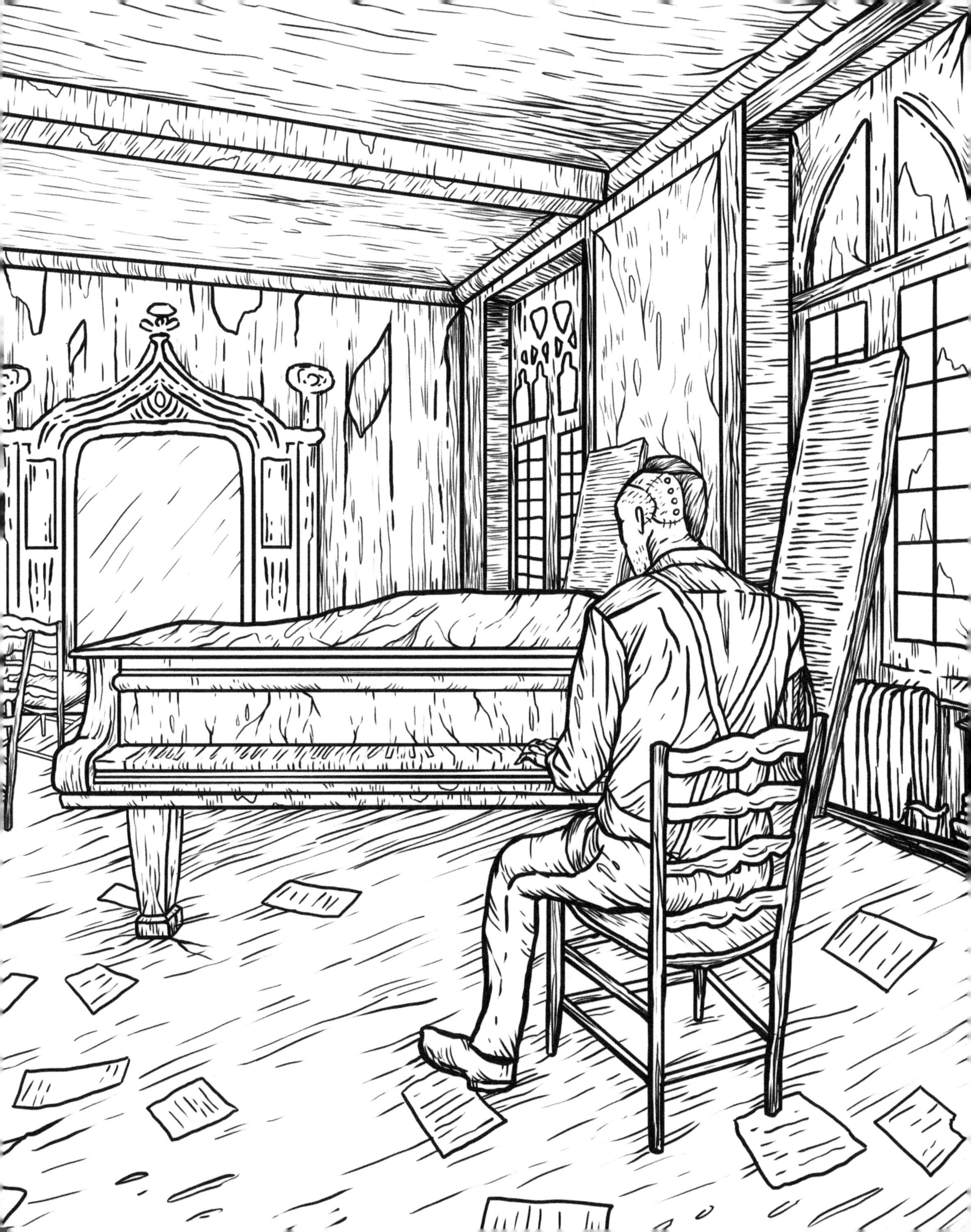

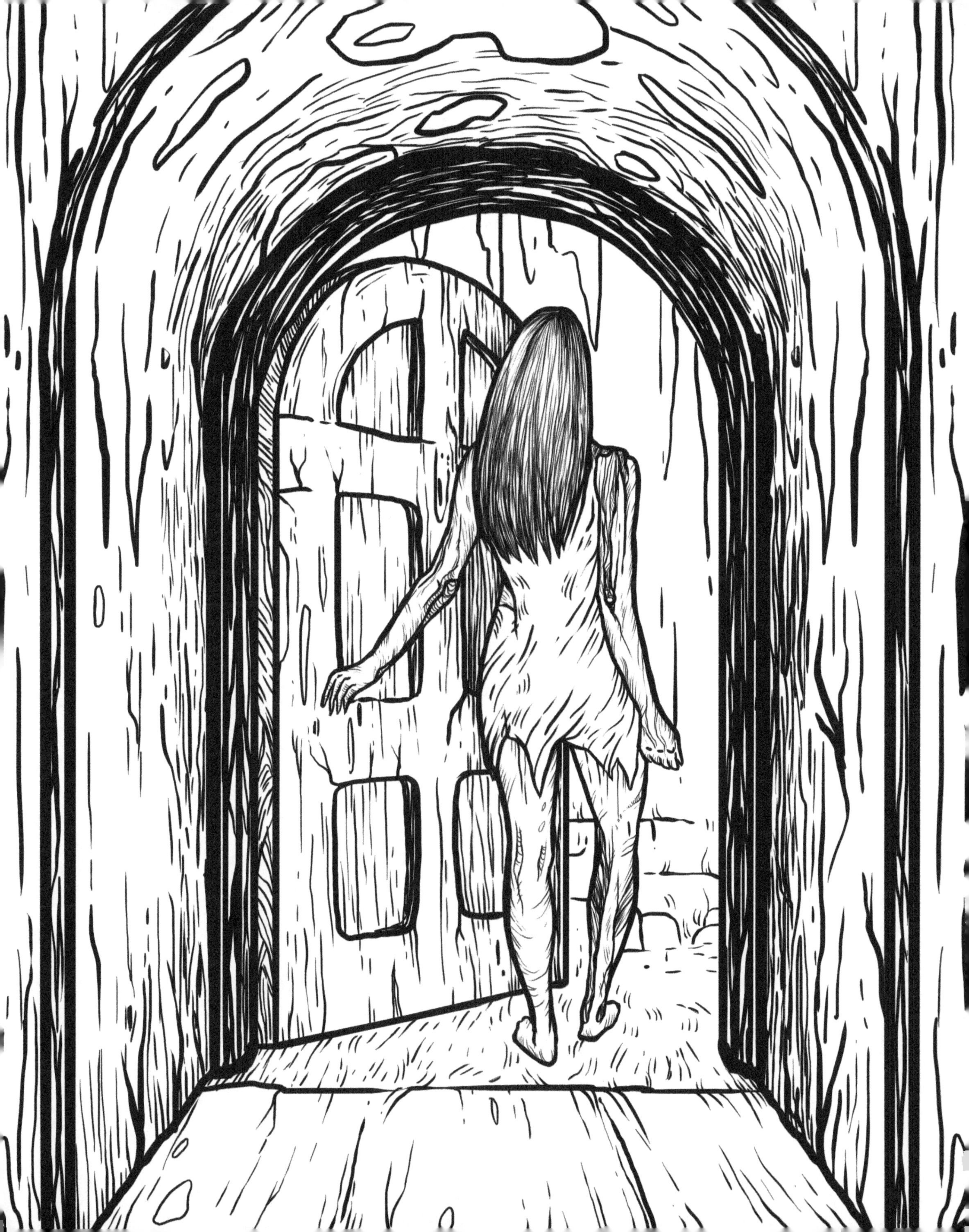